PRINCESS HEART

Princess Addison Gets ANGRY

by Molly Martin

pictures by Mélanie Florian

PICTURE WINDOW BOOKS

a capstone imprint

My name is Princess Addison
Lorelei Tiffany Genevieve Sinclair.

My mother calls me Addison.
My father calls me Honeyscoop.

My butlers call me
Your Highness.

My friends call me Addy.

But today, everyone calls me
Princess Angry.

And this is why . . .

Every morning, I take Ruffles
and Ribbons for a walk.
We run through the garden.

We dance by the fountain.

We pick hundreds of flowers
and carry them back to my room.

But not today.
Today it's raining!

I can't walk my dogs.
I can't run through the garden.
I can't dance by the fountain.
I can't pick flowers.

I feel like crying.
I feel like yelling.
I feel like hitting something.

I AM SO ANGRY!

My mother says
it's okay to feel
angry.

She says it's okay to cry.
It's okay to yell or shout.
It's okay to take a break
in your room.

But then she reminds me that
I am a princess.

A princess may get angry,
but a princess never hits people
or breaks things.

When a princess is angry,
she takes a deep breath.

She goes for a walk.

She reads a book.

She tells someone how angry she is feeling.

And soon enough, the angry feelings start to melt away.

A princess knows there is always tomorrow.

And tomorrow, it might not rain.

Princess Heart books are published by Picture Window Books
A Capstone Imprint
1710 Roe Crest Drive
North Mankato, Minnesota 56003
www.capstonepub.com

Library of Congress Cataloging-in-Publication Data
Martin, Molly, 1979-
Princess Addison gets angry / by Molly Martin ; illustrated by Melanie Florian.
p. cm. — (Princess heart)
Summary: Princess Addison is angry because it is raining
and she cannot go outside, but she knows what a
princess does to control her emotions.
ISBN 978-1-4048-7851-8 (library binding) -- ISBN 978-1-4048-8107-5 (paper over board)
1. Anger—Juvenile fiction. 2. Emotions--Juvenile fiction. 3. Princesses--Juvenile fiction.
[1. Anger--Fiction. 2. Emotions--Fiction. 3. Princesses--Fiction.] 1. Florian, Melanie, ill.
II. Title.
PZ7.M364128Pri 2013
813.6--dc23

2012026418

Image credits: Shutterstock/Pushkin (cover background)
Shutterstock/Kalenik Hanna (end sheets pattern)

Printed in the United States of America in Brainerd, Minnesota.
092012   006938BANGS13